STAR WARS™

THE FORCE AWAKENS

FINN'S STORY

WRITTEN BY JESSE J. HOLLAND

BASED ON THE SCREENPLAY BY
LAWRENCE KASDAN & J. J. ABRAMS
AND
MICHAEL ARNDT

D0289591

LOS ANGELES · NEW YORK

© & TM 2016 Lucasfilm Ltd.

All rights reserved. Published by Disney • Lucasfilm Press, an imprint of
Disney Book Group. No part of this book may be reproduced or transmitted in
any form or by any means, electronic or mechanical, including photocopying,
recording, or by any information storage and retrieval system, without
written permission from the publisher.

For information address Disney • Lucasfilm Press,
1101 Flower Street, Glendale, California 91201.

Printed in the United States of America

First Edition, September 2016

1 3 5 7 9 10 8 6 4 2

FAC-029261-16218

ISBN 978-1-4847-9022-9

Library of Congress Control Number on file

SUSTAINABLE
FORESTRY
INITIATIVE

Certified Sourcing

www.sfiprogram.org
SFI-01415

Cover and interior art by Brian Rood

Visit the official *Star Wars* website at: www.starwars.com.

CONTENTS

CHAPTER

I

THE STAR DESTROYER was silent as it glided through the blackness of space. But for stormtrooper FN-2187, the chatter around him was almost deafening as he nervously adjusted and readjusted his formfitting white armor.

FN-2187 had prepared long and hard for that day, but he couldn't stop sweating. Other stormtroopers were laughing and joking among themselves as they noisily prepared for their assignment. But FN-2187 couldn't bring himself to join in. He was too worried about what was going to happen during his first real assignment.

Even though they were all wearing identical

armor, FN-2187 could easily spot in the crowd his three friends who made up the FN Corps with him. Each stormtrooper had an assigned First Order designator, but when they were alone, the four of them used the nicknames they'd given each other and themselves.

FN-2199 was Nines, because he thought it sounded cool. Their sniper, FN-2000, called himself Zeroes, because of the pure simplicity of his designator. The three zeroes made him feel special, and he didn't care about the whispers that someone who called himself a zero wasn't going to have much expected of him. Zeroes liked it, and he stuck with it.

FN-2003 didn't get to pick his own nickname. He got stuck with Slip, because he was always sliding in behind everyone else. Slip was a bit slower, a tad clumsier, and a little less studious than the rest of their fire team. He tried hard, but he was never quite at the same level as the rest of the group.

And the rest of the group was never quite at

the same level as FN-2187. Everyone knew that he was one of the best stormtrooper cadets ever to have come through training, and next to him—especially in one-on-one training—most of the other cadets looked and sometimes felt more like Slip.

FN-2187 was strong, loyal, brave, smart, and willing to follow orders but able to make correct decisions on his own when he needed to. He was clear officer material for the First Order, so he had never been given a nickname and had never chosen one for himself.

After years of training, FN-2187 had itched for some real action. Like other stormtrooper cadets, he'd rotated through several lower level duties, including a janitorial assignment, but he hadn't seen any real live-fire action yet. Then one day their trainer and leader, Captain Phasma, told him that they would be deployed. So FN-2187 gathered his men, double-checked their gear, and headed to their transport.

"Did the captain say where we're going, what we're doing?" Slip asked once they were aboard and alone.

"Of course not," Zeroes said dismissively. "She's not going to tell stormtroopers the Supreme Leader's plans, or General Hux's, or even her own. She's not going to ask for our opinion. She's got a job she wants done and she's counting on us to do it."

Once their gear was stowed away and their helmets were off, they finally had time to chat with the older stormtroopers who shared their space.

"Fresh meat," said the stormtrooper across from them. "Who's who?"

Slip puffed up proudly. "FN Corps. Slip"— he pointed to himself and then around to the others—"Zeroes, Nines, and Eff-Enn-Two-One-Eight-Seven."

The stormtrooper looked FN-2187 in the eyes. "Let me guess. Eff-Enn-Two-One-Eight-Seven is in charge, right?"

"That's right."

The stormtrooper harrumphed and stared at FN-2187. "No nickname. You're one of those."

FN-2187 looked around at the others, confused. "One of those what?"

The stormtrooper chuckled, but there was something hard and dangerous in his laugh. It wasn't what you would call friendly. "An outsider, cadet. You're on the outside, and you'll always be looking in and wondering why you don't belong."

The rest of the stormtroopers laughed, including FN-2187's friends, which only intensified the bad feeling rising in the pit of his stomach.

A few hours later, they were marching through a mining colony called Pressy's Tumble to "restore order," as Captain Phasma coldly described it to them. Enemy agents were fomenting rebellion among the miners, who had been unearthing a valuable ore that was crucial to the First Order's plans. So FN-2187 and his troop had been told they were there to put an end to the disturbance and get everything back on schedule.

Once they were on the ground, Captain Phasma's icy voice crackled in FN-2187's helmet. "Proceed with your team to level alpha-seven-seven, room aught-three. Confirm."

"Confirmed."

A few minutes later, they approached Captain Phasma, who was standing outside a closed door, light glinting off her chrome armor. "The negotiators are inside," she said. "You and your team will accompany me."

The question escaped FN-2187's lips before he could stop it: "We're negotiating with the Republic?"

"No, for the striking miners." Phasma strode into the room and stood in front of a table with four humanoids.

A bedraggled human gathered his courage to speak. "Have you considered our requests?" He swallowed hard.

Phasma hesitated slightly. "I have given your request the thought it deserves." Her helmet turned slightly toward FN-2187, and her voice was thick with menace as she said, "Kill them."

Silence filled the room. No one moved, as if they couldn't believe what they had heard. FN-2187 was sure it was a mistake.

But then Slip fired, and then Zeroes, and then Nines.

When the blasts had ceased, Phasma walked across the room and nudged the bodies with her armored boot. Her dark cape flapped softly as she moved toward FN-2187 and stood in front of him.

"You're now stormtroopers." Phasma looked around at them, and they could hear pride in her voice.

Back on the Star Destroyer, Zeroes, Nines, and Slip celebrated their day's work with the other stormtroopers, but FN-2187 went his own way, saying he wanted to get more simulation time. No one objected.

FN-2187 asked the computer for a random scenario, and it obliged, allowing him to pick off Resistance fighters right and left. But then it started to mix in civilians, first as obstacles to be avoided but then as hidden Resistance fighters to be eliminated. Finally, there was no one in uniform to shoot. Instead, women and children filled his sights.

FN-2187 lowered his rifle.

This isn't right, he thought.

But what could he do?

CHAPTER
2

A FEW DAYS LATER, FN-2187 was aboard another transport ship. Captain Phasma had ordered his team to deploy to a desert planet called Jakku.

Stormtroopers marched out of their transports onto the sandy desert of Jakku. The ships had landed only a few klicks outside a small village.

None of the officers had told the stormtroopers exactly why they were there, only that there was something and someone in the village that the higher-ups wanted badly. As soon as the stormtroopers landed, Resistance fighters began to pepper them with small-arms fire. The stormtroopers' armor could deflect most of it, but they quickly cut down several of the village's ragtag defenders.

Before he could engage in the battle, FN-2187 saw Slip on the ground.

Slip's white armor had an ugly black scorch mark on the front. FN-2187 tried to lift his friend's head, but a pained groan made him stop.

Stunned silent, FN-2187 could only watch as Slip's body began to shudder, and with his last breath, his friend reached up to touch FN-2187's helmet, leaving a bloody mark on his visor.

FN-2187 backed away, speechless. *Did that really just happen?*

He didn't have much time to consider the question. Embers rained from the sky as fellow stormtroopers shoved him toward the center of the now-burning village. Meanwhile, a massive shuttle came in to land nearby.

It was Kylo Ren's shuttle.

Kylo Ren was the Supreme Leader's greatest warrior: a dark and powerful figure known for his erratic outbursts and fits of rage. Kylo stalked out of the ship and strode through the smoke and destruction the First Order had brought upon the village. The battle had ended, and surviving villagers, now prisoners, watched warily as the masked Kylo Ren approached an elderly man two troopers had dragged forward.

Tall and cloaked, with a black-and-silver mask and thick breathing apparatus, Kylo Ren exuded the same invincible confidence as Captain Phasma—only deadlier, if that was possible. Afraid to move, FN-2187 watched from the corner of his eye as Kylo Ren's distorted voice rose and fell in negotiation with the elderly leader.

Although the lenses of his helmet showed no difference between Kylo and the others, FN-2187 imagined a distinct aura surrounding the tall warrior, one that crackled with menace as he talked. Suddenly, FN-2187 saw Kylo's hand fly to his side, and the red flare of a lightsaber flashed against the night sky.

Without warning or mercy, Kylo Ren put an end to the old man.

Then FN-2187 heard the telltale crackle of blaster fire, but instead of an explosion, he saw Kylo raise his hand and, somehow, stop the bolt of energy in midair.

Stormtroopers ran to the source of the blast and dragged a Resistance pilot in front of Kylo. A kick to the legs drove the man to his knees, but it did not change the smirk on his face one bit. FN-2187 wanted to watch what came next, but a lieutenant told the remaining troopers to fall in and wait for orders.

FN-2187 gathered the surviving members of his fire team and stood at attention behind Kylo Ren, who whispered something to the Resistance pilot before two stormtroopers roughly took him by the arms and dragged him to the First Order transport. Captain Phasma approached Kylo.

"Sir, the villagers."

FN-2187 expected to be told to torch the buildings, destroying any chance of retaliation from the villagers before the First Order could leave orbit. But that was not what Kylo said.

"Kill them all."

A single nod and Phasma turned, looking directly at FN-2187 at the far end of the line of troopers. "On my command. Fire!"

In a single motion, the stormtroopers snapped their blasters up, took aim at the helpless crowd, and started shooting. But FN-2187 hesitated, then simply pretended to fire.

When the smoke cleared, only the First Order troopers and their superiors were left standing. Once again, it hadn't mattered that FN-2187 never pulled his trigger. The villagers were still dead.

FN-2187 looked around in a quiet panic and, to his horror, made eye contact with Kylo Ren himself. The dark cloaked figure stared right at the frozen trooper.

He knows. He must know. And I'm ... dead.

But he wasn't. The glance, which seemed to FN-2187 to last an eternity, lasted barely a second. Then Kylo Ren resumed his pace, looking deep in thought as he strode toward his shuttle.

When Kylo had passed, the blue bolt of blaster fire that had been suspended in midair was finally freed from the dark warrior's hold. The blast made contact with a vaporator in the middle of the village and exploded in a shower of sparks.

As troopers razed the wreckage with flamethrowers, FN-2187 took one last look at Slip.

Slip had died for nothing. Even worse, his death had come as they were terrorizing and killing innocent people. That wasn't what they had trained for. The First Order was supposed to represent peace and stability, not fear and death.

I can't do this anymore, he thought.

THE FIRST ORDER TROOP transports touched down gently in the landing bay of a Star Destroyer known as the *Finalizer.* Stormtroopers disembarked in waves, marching in squads through the hangar. FN-2187 staggered out of his transport, with Zeroes and Nines close behind.

A fellow stormtrooper dragged the captured Resistance pilot off another ship and led him right past FN-2187. FN-2187 felt a twinge of sympathy for the prisoner, but his mind was too consumed by his own predicament to really focus on anything else.

For a second time, he had disobeyed

direct orders. He knew what happened to stormtroopers who were disobedient.

FN-2187 was starting to panic again.

He needed to breathe—to *really* breathe, not just recirculate his own oxygen through the filters his helmet provided.

FN-2187 climbed into an empty transport ship and removed the black-and-white weight from his head.

But his panting only continued. He couldn't steady his heartbeat.

What am I going to do?

Slip and the villagers returned to his mind. A wave of nausea flooded his body.

"Eff-Enn-Two-One-Eight-Seven. Submit your blaster for inspection."

Phasma's cold metallic voice broke the silence of the transport.

FN-2187 looked over his shoulder, startled by her presence.

"Yes, Captain."

This was only a reprieve, and a short one at that. He was still in danger, but at least now FN-2187 would get a few more moments before the inevitable happened.

"And who gave you permission to remove that helmet?" Her tone held the promise of punishment.

"I'm sorry, Captain."

He couldn't look at her. She would see right through him.

"Report to my division at once," Phasma said as she left the transport, her boots pounding hard against the grated floor.

FN-2187's time was officially up. If he turned over his weapon to Phasma, the scans would show that he had disobeyed orders, and he would be punished. If he didn't turn over the weapon immediately, she would assume that he had done something to disguise what the rifle would have shown, and he would be punished. If he didn't show up at Phasma's division within the next few moments, she would send some of her personal guards after him and he would be punished.

FN-2187 was in a bind.

He needed help.

But who would help him?

Everyone on the Star Destroyer was allegiant to the First Order.

Well, FN-2187 thought, *not exactly everyone . . .*

FN-2187 took a deep breath as he approached the cell. Once he entered, there would be no turning back. It was now or never. Confidence was key. He kept his stride steady, and the heavy door opened before him.

A single guard stood near the door, and in the center of the room, shackled and slumped down in an interrogation chair, was the Resistance pilot. The cuts and bruises on his face showed that he'd been beaten, and the haunted look he gave FN-2187 told him the man had nearly given up.

FN-2187 turned to the guard. "Ren wants the prisoner."

The restraints clamped to the pilot's arms and legs suddenly sprang free, and FN-2187 escorted the weakened prisoner out the door.

FN-2187 marched the pilot through the sleek hallways of the Star Destroyer with his blaster pressed firmly to the man's side. He hoped Kylo Ren hadn't permanently damaged the guy, because the next part of his plan required a pilot.

"Turn here."

FN-2187 pushed the prisoner into a cramped passageway off to the side.

From the Resistance pilot's eyes, FN-2187 could tell that he thought he was being led to his doom. He had to speak quickly to gain the man's trust.

"Listen carefully. If you do exactly as I say, I can get you out of here."

"What?" The pilot stared back at him blankly.

FN-2187 took off his helmet. He needed the Resistance fighter to understand. They didn't have much time before someone noticed the pilot was missing.

"This is a rescue. I'm helping you escape," he hissed.

The pilot wasn't convinced. "You with the Resistance?"

FN-2187 couldn't help snorting at the ridiculous notion. "What? No, no, no, I'm breaking you out. Can you fly a TIE fighter?"

The prisoner's exhausted expression melted away. "I can fly anything." He looked FN-2187 up and down. "Why are you helping me?"

FN-2187 stood a little taller. "Because it's the right thing to do," he said.

The pilot instantly saw through his act. "You need a pilot."

FN-2187 sighed. "I need a pilot."

The prisoner just smiled. "We're going to do this."

FN-2187 put on his helmet, turned the pilot back around, and marched him toward the landing bay. Now all they had to do was make it through hundreds of First Order troops without suspicion, get to a TIE fighter, and escape the First Order.

CHAPTER
4

FN-2187 AND THE RESISTANCE PILOT
entered the hangar bay, which was teeming with
people.

"Okay, stay calm, stay calm," FN-2187
whispered as he poked the Resistance fighter
with his blaster.

"I am calm," the pilot whispered back.

"I'm talking to myself," FN-2187 replied.

Finally, they made it to a two-man TIE fighter
and dropped inside.

"I always wanted to fly one of these things,"
the pilot said almost reverently. He looked over
his shoulder at FN-2187. "Can you shoot?"

FN-2187 removed his helmet. He was happy to be rid of it, he hoped once and for all.

But he had never been in a TIE fighter before.

The pilot began to call out instructions as FN-2187 felt the ship thrum to life.

"Use the toggle on the left to switch between missiles, cannons, and magpulse. Use the sight on the right to aim. Triggers to fire."

FN-2187 was completely lost. "This is very complicated," he confessed as the TIE fighter lurched forward.

But the ship was still attached to its docking station by a thick cable.

"I can fix this," the pilot called over the sound of alarms.

All around them, First Order troops started to notice. Stormtroopers reached for their blasters and began to pepper the TIE with fire.

FN-2187 started firing back, at the walls of the landing bay, the troops on the ground, neighboring ships—really anything he could identify and target. One final volley took out the control room, allowing his pilot to release the TIE fighter's docking cable and dart out into open space.

"This thing really moves!" The pilot was clearly in his element as he maneuvered the TIE under the belly of the Star Destroyer. "All right, we gotta take out as many of these cannons as we can or we're not going to get very far. I'm going to get us in position. Just stay sharp."

The TIE fighter dodged blaster fire, and the pilot turned the ship toward the *Finalizer's* massive bank of cannons.

"Up ahead! Up ahead! You see it? I've got us dead centered. It's a clean shot!"

"Okay, got it!" FN-2187 fired a spurt of green blasts and the cannons blew up in a shower of sparks.

"Yeah!" FN-2187 cheered as their TIE sailed

through the flames. "Did you see that? Did you see that?"

"I saw it!" the Resistance fighter replied. "Hey, what's your name?"

"Eff-Enn-Two-One-Eight-Seven!" the trooper answered, still focused on the task at hand.

"Eff-wha?"

FN-2187 shrugged. "That's the only name they ever gave me."

He could see the pilot shaking his head in disgust. "Well, I ain't using it. Eff-Enn, huh? Finn. I'm going to call you Finn. Is that all right?"

"Finn," FN-2187 said out loud. It would be a new name for a new start. "Yeah. Finn. I like that!"

The Resistance pilot introduced himself as Poe Dameron, but there was no time for chitchat. The First Order had fired a deadly blast from the ventral cannon, and Finn and Poe had to work together to outmaneuver and shoot down the blast.

Finn noticed that Poe had turned the ship back toward Jakku.

"No, no, no! We can't go back to Jakku. We need to get out of this system!" Finn shouted.

Poe shook his head. "I've got to get my droid before the First Order does."

Finn couldn't believe what he was hearing. "What? *A droid?*"

"That's right," Poe replied as he dodged cannon fire. "He's a BB unit. Orange and white. One of a kind."

"I don't care what color he is!" Finn yelled. "No droid can be that important. We've got to get as far away from the First Order as we can! We go back to Jakku, we die!"

Poe wouldn't listen. "That droid has a map that leads straight to Luke Skywalker."

Now Finn *really* couldn't believe his ears. "Oh, you've gotta be kidding me!"

But before Finn could say another word, a powerful blast hit their TIE fighter. The ship spiraled out of control, toward the sandy planet below, and there was nothing Finn or Poe could do to stop it.

Finn opened his eyes with a start. He was lying on the ground, strapped to his ejection seat and sweating under the hot desert sun.

When he staggered to his feet and looked around, there was only a vast ocean of sandy dunes in every direction, except for a small plume of black smoke rising in the distance. Finn stumbled toward the smoke.

"Poe!" Finn called expectantly as he followed the debris field to the downed TIE fighter.

Flames licked at the ship as he peered into the cockpit. Finn could barely make something out in the smoke-filled wreckage.

He reached in and pulled out Poe's brown leather jacket, but before he could search the rest of the cockpit, he heard a strange groaning sound and the sand began to sink beneath him.

Finn quickly stepped back, staring, dumb-founded, as the sand dune swallowed the TIE whole.

And just when he thought the day couldn't get any stranger . . . *BOOM!*

The sand erupted before him in one gigantic satisfied belch.

Finn was all alone.

But if he stayed there, the First Order would soon be upon him. There was no choice. He had to keep moving.

CHAPTER
5

A FEW HOURS LATER, Finn was dejected, disoriented, and exhausted. Endless sand surrounded him in every direction, and he had no idea where he was. The sun burned him as he trudged up and down the enormous dunes.

Along the way, Finn had shed his white stormtrooper armor bit by bit. He had no use for the former symbol of his allegiance to the First Order. It was only weighing him down now, and he was glad when he threw off the last piece of it.

It was fortunate he had kept Poe's jacket, because that was all he had to shield his head and eyes from the glare of the sun. Then again, his black shirt and pants did little to ward off the heat. Parched and on the verge of sunstroke, all he could do was continue to shuffle forward, hoping upon hope that he would find someone, somewhere, or something before his otherwise inevitable death.

Finn panted heavily as he climbed another massive dune, the sun blinding him as he crested it. But as his eyes adjusted to the glare, he noticed a small settlement below.

Finn tried to laugh, but his parched throat would only make croaking sounds. Moving as fast as his dehydrated body would take him, he stumbled toward the outpost.

To Finn, it looked more like a junkyard than a spaceport, but at that point he couldn't afford to be choosy. A large outdoor market with loud merchants hawking all kinds of merchandise caught Finn's attention and raised his hopes of finding something to drink.

But as he staggered through tented stalls and pleaded for something to quench his overwhelming thirst, scavengers, traders, and thieves looked at him with little sympathy.

"Water . . . water," Finn begged, but the merchants pushed him out of the way, most of them with a curse or two, in favor of paying customers.

Finn was just about to give up all hope when he heard the beautiful sounds of sloshing behind him. He whirled around and saw a trough with a big slobbering happabore drinking from it.

Finn ran toward the trough and drew the brackish water to his mouth over and over again, trying not to gag. The happabore was not too happy about sharing, though, and suddenly used his large snout to knock Finn to the ground with a harrumph.

Finn was startled by the creature, but he was even more surprised to hear the crashing sounds of a struggle inside the market. Finn hoped it wasn't stormtroopers. When he looked closer, he saw that it wasn't the First Order.

It was a girl, and she was fighting off two attackers.

Finn ran forward, ready to defend the girl, but he quickly realized that she didn't need his help. Dressed in the light-colored desert garb of the locals, the girl whirled a heavy staff like a pro. With just a few moves, both attackers were lying still in the sand.

Finn was impressed, and he looked around to see if anyone else was watching this girl beating two fools into the dirt. No one seemed fazed by it, though. Finn concluded that this must be a rough kind of village.

The girl, still breathing hard, removed a tarp that the attackers had thrown over a small droid. It was an orange-and-white BB unit.

The droid took notice of Finn and exclaimed something to the girl in binary. All of a sudden, the girl charged madly toward him, quarterstaff held threateningly.

After witnessing the girl's fighting skills firsthand, Finn decided his best bet would be simply to run.

Dodging around tents and pushing aside onlookers, Finn ran as fast as he could through the market. Ducking into a tent, he chanced a look back to see whether he'd lost the girl. No one was there.

Thwack!

The girl stepped in front of him and used her staff to slam him painfully to the ground.

"What's your hurry, thief?" she growled.

Just then, the little BB unit rolled up to them. Easing around the girl, the droid extended a live electrical circuit and gave Finn a harsh jolt.

"Ow! Hey! What?" Finn sputtered, swatting at the little droid, who skittered behind the girl.

"The jacket. This droid says you stole it," the girl insisted.

Finn looked down at the leather jacket he was wearing. He'd completely forgotten he had Poe's jacket on.

"I've had a pretty messed-up day, all right? So I'd appreciate it if you'd stop accusing me— *Ow!* Stop it!"

The little droid had zapped him again. He was small, but man, was he tough.

"Then where'd you get it?" she asked. "It belongs to his master."

That was when it all started making sense. Finn couldn't believe it, though. Out of all the places on that planet, he had happened to stumble on the village where *Poe Dameron's droid* was hiding?

Finn sighed. "It belonged to Poe Dameron. That was his name, right?"

The droid looked at Finn, then at the girl, then back at Finn. He looked almost hopeful, if a droid could even be such a thing. Finn felt terrible about what he had to say next.

"He was captured by the First Order. I helped him escape, but our ship crashed. Poe didn't make it."

The little droid's head hung low.

"Look, I tried to help him. I'm sorry," Finn said as the droid slowly rolled away.

The girl watched the droid and then turned to look at Finn. "So you're with the Resistance?"

Finn met her gaze and noticed that she was quite pretty when she wasn't hitting him with her staff. He wanted to be honest with her, but what would she think of him if she knew that he had been a stormtrooper?

"Obviously," he lied as he stood from the sand. Then he dropped his voice low, attempting to sound both brave and secretive. "Yes, I am. I'm with the Resistance. Yeah, I am *with* the Resistance."

"I've never met a Resistance fighter before," she admitted.

Finn nodded. "Well, this is what we look

like. Some of us." Not wanting to dig himself too deep into detail, he added, "Others look different."

The young woman gestured in the direction the little droid had rolled. "Beebee-Ate says he's on a secret mission; he has to get back to your base."

Finn nodded, thinking of the last words Poe had said to him. "Apparently he has a map that leads to Luke Skywalker, and everyone's after it."

"Luke Skywalker?" The young woman's voice was filled with awe. "I thought he was a myth."

CHAPTER
6

FINN AND THE GIRL didn't have much time to discuss the whereabouts of the missing Jedi, though, because BB-8 had rolled up, beeping at them like mad. The young woman seemed to be able to understand the little droid. Beckoning Finn to follow her, she peeked around a tent corner. Looking over her shoulder, Finn saw what had caused so much commotion from the little droid: stormtroopers!

Finn knew they had only seconds before the stormtroopers spotted them. They had to run—right away!

Out of pure instinct, Finn reached down and

grabbed the young woman's hand, then pulled her to concealment in a nearby tent.

The girl was confused. "What are you doing?"

"Come on!" Finn yelled as he dragged her away from the laser fire that ripped through the tent they had just vacated. "Come on, Beebee-Ate!"

Holding hands, they zigzagged through the market, dodging behind tents and around stacked containers. The young woman tried to pull her hand free from Finn's, but he refused to let her go. If they separated, he'd lose both her and the droid. She might know the market, but that wouldn't matter if a whole squadron of trained stormtroopers was on its way.

"Let go of me! I know how to run without you holding my hand!" she shouted over the laser fire. She freed her hand and gestured toward a nearby tent. "Beebee-Ate, stay close. This way."

They darted into a tent for a momentary respite. Silently, they waited to see if the stormtroopers were nearby. Breathing heavily, the young woman looked accusingly at Finn. "They're shooting at both of us!"

Finn searched the tent for a blaster. "Yeah, they saw you with me! You're marked!"

She glared at him. "Well, thanks for that!" she said sarcastically.

"I'm not the one who chased *you* down with a stick," he reminded her.

While they talked, a familiar whine was rising in the background of the market. Having heard the sound in hundreds of simulations, Finn knew what was about to happen and that they had only seconds left to live if they didn't move immediately. Grabbing the young woman's hand again, he dashed out of the tent and sprinted with her across the plaza.

"Stop taking my hand!" she shouted as she ran to keep up. But he didn't have time to argue. Looking over his shoulder, he could see twin TIE fighters screaming over the town. Before they could take more than a few steps, the TIE fighters' blasters opened fire and Finn felt the impact throw him into the air.

A few seconds later, the young woman was shaking him, looking concerned. He focused on her face. "Are you okay?" Finn asked.

She gave him a look of slight surprise, as if she'd never heard those words before.

"Yeah," she said, and held her hand out to help him up. Grateful, he took it and didn't let go. She began to pull him across the plaza toward the spaceport. "Follow me!"

They sprinted across the sand as the TIE fighters blasted the market again and again, trying to flush them out. They needed to choose a ship and attempt to get away.

"We can't outrun them," Finn wheezed.

The young woman pointed toward a parked four-engine ship a few landing pads down. "We might in that quadjumper," she shouted over the screaming TIE fighters.

"We need a pilot!" Finn shouted.

The young woman smiled. "We've got one," she said proudly.

Finn shook his head. *She's a pilot, too?*

Another ship, an old YT cargo ship half hidden under some kind of covering, was much closer. They could be on board in seconds, instead of having to continue their headlong dash out in the open. "What about that ship?" he asked.

"That one's garbage!" she shouted back.

But seconds later, the TIE fighters quickly turned their quadjumper into a massive fireball, stopping them short. Finn and the young woman looked at each other for a second.

"The garbage'll do!" she screamed, and they turned and ran for the old ship.

CHAPTER
7

FINN, BB-8, and the young woman dashed up the ramp and through the dank hallways of the old cargo ship. The girl ran toward the cockpit and gestured at a small ladder. "Gunner position's down there!"

"You ever fly this thing?" he asked as he climbed down into the gunport.

"No! This ship hasn't flown in years," she shouted back.

"Great," Finn said to himself as he slid into the antiquated gunner's seat. He'd only ever been in the one TIE fighter, but he could tell that the First Order technology was far beyond what lay before him now. Instead of using readouts and targeting computers, like a TIE fighter, this ship required him to manually swing the guns into position by swiveling his seat. A control stalk maneuvered him and the guns 360 degrees. He just had to press two red buttons and they'd be in business—if they ever got off the ground.

"I can do this," he whispered to himself.

Finn felt the ship's engines shudder and roar to life. He was momentarily gratified to see that his pilot was able to steer them into the bright Jakku sky. But then he realized what she was probably thinking, and he knew he had to stop her from heading into the upper atmosphere, where more TIE fighters and the *Finalizer* were no doubt waiting for them.

Finn pulled on a comm set.

"Stay low! Stay low!" Finn shouted. "It'll confuse their tracking systems."

Finn heard the young woman call out to the droid, "Beebee-Ate! Hold on! I'm going low!"

Seconds later, the ship banked in a giant arc and soared across the sands of Jakku, within meters of the two incoming TIEs.

Finn tried to get his breath back under control as the ship shook and rocked from TIE fighter fire.

"What are you doing back there?" called the girl. "Are you ever going to fire back?"

Finn's seat bucked like a wild bantha with each direct hit. "I'm working on it!"

Leaning left and right, Finn swung the cannons toward the TIE fighters and pressed down on the fire buttons. The guns spit red laser fire at the TIE fighters, which nimbly dodged out of the way. Again and again, Finn fired, but he couldn't lock on to the ships with the bobbing and weaving his pilot was putting them through.

"We need cover, quick!" Finn shouted into his headset.

"We're about to get some . . . I hope," she answered.

Finn peered out of the gunport at the hulking wrecks they were heading toward and realized his pilot meant to take them into a starship graveyard. Giant Star Destroyers and rebel battle cruisers were everywhere, the remnants of a long-ago war.

"Come on, come on," he muttered as the ship banked hard left and furrowed a row in the desert sands. The crazy maneuver placed one of the TIE fighters directly in his sights, and Finn blasted the ship into smoky bits that scattered across the sands.

"Nice shot," he heard through his headset.

Finn puffed up a bit at the praise. "I am getting pretty good at this." He smiled.

But just then, the remaining TIE fighter rocked Finn's turret with laser fire. Finn pulled and jerked at his controls, but the cannon was jammed and refused to move.

Finn realized they were now defenseless.

"The cannon's stuck in forward position. I can't move it!" said Finn. "You've got to lose him!"

The ship weaved even more as the TIE fighter's green laser fire got closer and closer. No matter how close they flew to the ground or how tightly the young woman maneuvered against the rusted starship hulls, the TIE pilot wouldn't give up.

Suddenly, the hollowed-out hull of a crashed Super Star Destroyer loomed in front of Finn's window.

"Get ready," shouted the girl.

Ready? Ready for what?

He felt the ship bank and career down, angling for a rear exhaust port of the Super Star Destroyer. She wasn't thinking about taking them in there, was she?

"Are we really doing this?" Finn shouted.

For what seemed like an eternity, the two ships dangerously raced through the Destroyer, the freighter not able to make any ground and the TIE fighter not able to line up any successful shots.

Just when it seemed like they were going to

be blasted to bits, his pilot whipped them out of a narrow hole in the side of the Super Star Destroyer. Finn was thrown back roughly as the freighter leaped straight up into the sky and flipped upside down so that the pursuing TIE fighter was right in front of the forward-locked cannon. Finn grinned and fired.

The TIE fighter exploded in a shower of sparks.

Finn cheered as the pilot angled their ship toward the blackness of space. Stripping himself of his restraints in the gunner's seat, Finn watched briefly as the sandy planet of Jakku became smaller and smaller in the viewport.

The last time he'd left that planet, he thought he was flying to his doom. This time, he'd fought his way to freedom from the First Order, made a new friend, and found a valuable droid, and he was picking up a mission for the Resistance that could change the course of the galaxy.

Not bad for a few days' work.

FINN RAN TOWARD THE COCKPIT

only to almost collide with the pilot, who was rushing back to celebrate. Words of praise exploded from both of them.

"That was some flying! How did you do that?" Finn couldn't believe they'd pulled off the last maneuver.

"I—I'm not sure," she stammered excitedly. "I've flown smaller ships, but I've never left the planet."

Finn couldn't believe it. "No one trained you? That was amazing!"

The young woman blushed slightly and

smiled. "And you? Your last shot was dead-on. You got him in one blast!"

Finn smiled back with a hint of self-satisfaction. "You set me up for it . . . but that was pretty good, wasn't it?"

Their words faded away into silence as they continued to smile at each other. It had been a while since Finn had felt that comfortable with another person, and he could see she felt the same way.

BB-8 soon rolled into the corridor and began to chirp at the pilot with some urgency.

"You're okay," said the girl, kneeling in front of the little droid. "He's with the Resistance. He's going to get you home. We both will."

The lie burned inside Finn. *Why did I have to say that?*

The young woman straightened up and looked at Finn. "I don't know your name."

Finn realized that he didn't know hers, either. "Finn. What's yours?"

"I'm Rey," she replied with a smile.

Finn had to tell her the truth. She was too nice to be lied to.

"Rey . . ." Finn started, but before he could get anything else out, an explosion in the lounge startled both of them. Rey pointed to a floor grate that was gushing steam, and they rushed over to pull it free.

Rey leaped below to check things out, leaving Finn alone with BB-8 to wonder what had happened.

A few seconds later, Rey's head popped back up. She had a panicked look on her face. "It's the motivator. Grab me a Harris wrench, it's in there." She pointed to a storage box behind him.

Finn had no clue what a motivator was. Or a Harris wrench, for that matter. "How bad is it?" he asked as he searched through the various tools.

Her answer wasn't promising. "If we want to live, not good."

Finn grew anxious. "They're hunting us now and we've got to get out of this system!"

"Beebee-Ate said the location of the Resistance base is 'need to know,'" Rey replied. "If I'm taking you there, I *need* to know!"

Finn tossed the wrench he had found to Rey and then motioned for the little droid to roll toward him. If he could convince BB-8 to tell them where the base was, they'd all be safe from the First Order. And Poe's mission to get the map to the Resistance would be complete. All he needed to do was get the little droid to cooperate.

"You gotta tell us where your base is," he pleaded.

BB-8 shook his head and beeped at Finn accusingly.

Finn looked at the droid blankly. "I don't speak that."

He might not have understood what BB-8 said, but he knew it wasn't good. However, this was their only chance at survival. Finn was going to have to be completely honest with the little droid.

"All right, between us, I'm not with the Resistance, okay?"

BB-8 rolled back from Finn, clearly offended and skeptical.

"I'm just trying to get away from the First Order," Finn continued. "But you tell us where your base is, I'll get you there first. Deal?"

BB-8 tilted his head to the side, as though weighing his options.

"Droid, please!" Finn begged.

Just then, Rey's head appeared again from the floor. "Pilex driver, hurry!"

Finn went back to the box of tools. *Pilex driver?*

"So where's your base?" asked Rey.

Finn gave the droid a desperate look over his shoulder. "Go on, Beebee-Ate, tell her."

BB-8 looked back and forth from Finn to Rey.

Back and forth. Back and forth. The moment felt like an eternity.

"Please!" Finn whispered to the droid.

Finally, BB-8 issued a series of beeps toward Rey.

"The Ileenium system?" Rey looked confused.

"Yeah, the Ileenium system, that's the one. Get us there as fast as you can."

Finn played along as he tossed her the tool she needed.

Rey returned to her work, and Finn turned to smile at the droid, giving him a thumbs-up. The droid, using a welding torch, returned the gesture.

"I'll drop you two at Ponemah Terminal. I need the bonding tape, hurry!" said Rey.

"What about you?" Finn asked as he searched for the tape.

"I gotta get back to Jakku," Rey replied as though that were the most obvious fact in the galaxy.

"Back to Jak—why does everyone want to go back to Jakku? That place is—"

But Rey cut him off. Finn was having zero luck finding the bonding tape and she had needed it two minutes prior.

"It's not that one. No. No. The one I'm pointing to," Rey instructed as Finn fumbled with various spools of tape.

"No. No. No! If we don't patch this up, the propulsion tank will overflow and flood the ship with poisonous gas!" Rey exclaimed.

BB-8 needed to intervene. He rolled over and inclined his head directly above the spool of yellow tape Rey was pointing to.

"This?" Finn asked, picking up the tape.

"Yes." Rey breathed a sigh of relief as Finn tossed it to her, and she got back to work.

Finn still didn't understand why Rey would want to go back to Jakku, of all planets. He inched over to where Rey was working down below.

"Hey, Rey, you're a pilot. You can fly anywhere. Why go back?" Finn asked. "You got a family? Got a boyfriend? A cute boyfriend?" he added quickly.

"None of your business, that's why," Rey said sharply.

Just then, the lights inside the ship shut off and Finn felt the engines power down.

"That can't be good," Finn whispered.

"No, it can't be," Rey agreed as they ran toward the cockpit. Rey climbed into the pilot's chair, toggled a couple of switches, and then sat back in frustration.

"Someone's locked on to us," she said. "All controls are overridden."

An odd mechanical noise reverberated through the ship. It sounded as though it came from above them.

Finn climbed up onto the copilot's seat to look out the window, pressing his hand on top of Rey's head to steady himself.

"Get off," Rey grumbled. "Get off!"

But Finn was too terrified to take any notice. Bathed in red light, all he could see was the outline of a massive ship swallowing them into its hangar bay.

He sagged back in his seat, stunned. "It's the First Order," he whispered.

"What do we do?" Rey asked. "There must be something."

If only they hadn't been distracted by the repairs, they might have been able to make a jump to lightspeed.

The repairs! The propulsion tank! Finn knew what they could do.

"You said poisonous gas . . ." Finn prompted.

"I fixed that!" Rey snapped.

"Can you unfix it?"

Rey stared at Finn for a second, but she quickly understood his plan. They could flood the ship with poisonous gas, taking out any stormtroopers who tried to board. They rushed back to the lounge and grabbed some gas masks. Finn climbed below the floor grating.

"Come on, Beebee-Ate." Rey encouraged him as she led the droid to where Finn was standing.

"I got him," Finn said as he pulled the droid into the space below. But the little guy was much heavier than Finn had expected and nearly knocked the wind out of him.

"I'm okay," Finn exhaled. "Beebee-Ate, get off me."

BB-8 burbled to himself as Rey dropped in and pulled the grate over their hiding space. Then Rey started fiddling with some wires. "Do you think this will work on the stormtroopers?" she asked.

"Yeah, their masks filter out smoke. Not toxins," Finn answered, realizing that he sounded a bit too knowledgeable on the subject.

She was still working when they heard the heavy blast door of the ship open above them.

Then there were footfalls. But they didn't sound to Finn like the heavy boots of stormtroopers.

Either way, they had run out of time. Someone or something ripped away the grate above them. They were trapped.

CHAPTER
9

FINN AND REY were surprised to see an older man and a Wookiee standing above them. Where were the stormtroopers?

"Where are the others? Where's the pilot?" the man asked.

"I'm the pilot," Rey replied, still wearing her breathing apparatus.

The man looked at her unbelievingly. "You?" The Wookiee roared.

"No, it's true!" Rey answered the Wookiee. "We're the only ones on board."

"You can understand that thing?" Finn asked, surprised.

The man snorted. "And 'that thing' can understand you, too, so watch it.

"Come on out of there," he said, lowering his blaster and gesturing to them to climb out of the hole. "Where'd you get this ship?"

"Niima Outpost," answered Rey.

"Jakku?" The man sounded surprised. "That junkyard?"

"Thank you!" Finn exclaimed, giving Rey a glance. *"Junkyard."*

The man turned to the Wookiee. "Told you we should've double-checked the Western Reaches. Who had it, Ducain?"

"I stole it," Rey blurted out. "From Unkar Plutt. He stole it from the Irving Boys, who stole it from Ducain."

"Who stole it from me!" the man added angrily. "Well, you tell him that Han Solo just stole back the *Millennium Falcon* . . . for good."

Rey was in awe. "This is the *Millennium Falcon*? You're Han Solo?"

"I used to be," Han answered, wandering down the corridors of his old ship.

"Han Solo the Rebellion general?" Finn asked.

Rey looked at Finn as if he were insane. "No, the smuggler!" she said, correcting him.

Finn turned to the Wookiee. Surely that guy would have an answer. "Wasn't he a war hero?"

But the Wookiee just shrugged.

Rey was still starstruck. "This is the ship that made the Kessel Run in fourteen parsecs!"

"Twelve," Han boomed. He had walked through the ship and was returning to confront Rey and Finn.

"Hey, some moof-milker put a compressor on the ignition line."

"Unkar Plutt did," said Rey. "I thought it was a mistake, too. Puts too much stress on the—"

"Hyperdrive." Han finished her sentence with her.

He seemed a little impressed by Rey's

knowledge, but that obviously wasn't going to stop him from kicking them off his ship. "Chewie, throw them in a pod. We'll drop them at the nearest inhabited planet," Han ordered as he walked off.

"Wait! No!" Rey cried, following close behind. "We need your help."

"My help?" Han clearly did not like the taste those words left in his mouth.

"This droid has to get to the Resistance base as soon as possible!" explained Rey.

"He's carrying a map to Luke Skywalker," Finn chimed in, close at their heels.

Han froze in his tracks. He turned, his face somber. Finn hadn't meant to cause the old man pain, but Han needed to know how important this was.

"You *are* the Han Solo that fought with the Rebellion," said Finn. "You knew him."

Han nodded ever so slightly. "Yeah, I knew him. I knew Luke."

They were all silent for a moment, but the silence was broken by a distant metallic *ka-chunk* outside the *Millennium Falcon*.

Han looked exasperated. "Don't tell me a rathtar's gotten loose," he said, rushing off the *Falcon* into what Finn now recognized as an enormous commercial freighter. Chewie, Finn, Rey, and BB-8 followed at his heels

"Wait, what? Did you just say 'rathtars'?" Finn exclaimed. "Hey! You're not hauling rathtars on this freighter, are you?"

Han nodded. "I'm hauling rathtars," he said as he activated a panel of screens that showed different images from around the ship. One of the screens showed a transport vessel docking with their ship.

"Oh, great! It's the Guavian Death Gang, must have tracked us from Nantoon," Han said.

Rey looked at Han and Finn. "What's a rathtar?"

Han walked down a long narrow hallway

lined with cargo containers as he explained. "They're big and dangerous. I got three of them going to King Prana."

Finn went weak in the knees. "Three! How did you get them on board?"

Han sighed. "Used to have a bigger crew," he admitted before opening a hatch in the floor for them to hide under. "Get below and stay there until I say so. And don't even think about taking the *Falcon*."

"What about Beebee-Ate?" Rey asked.

"He stays with me until I get rid of the gang, then you can have him back and be on your way."

"What about the rathtars, where are you keeping 'em?" Finn asked just as a terrifying *THWACK* answered him. A slimy, thick tentacle had hit the window of a cargo container behind them.

"There's one," Han said as Finn backed away and started scrambling down through the open hatch.

Rey looked concerned about Han, but Finn was concerned about them.

"What are you going to do?" Rey asked.

Han just smiled. "Same thing I always do, talk my way out of it."

Chewie let out a moan of disagreement.

"Yes I do," Han replied. "Every time."

Finn didn't know which one of them was right, but at least someone had a plan.

CHAPTER
10

FINN AND REY were jammed together under the floor of a ship once more. Finn could hear Han trying to negotiate his way out of his predicament. But things weren't going well for the smuggler.

"Han Solo, you're a dead man," said the Guavian Death Gang's leader, Bala-Tik.

That silver tongue Han had boasted of earlier didn't seem to be working. Beside Finn, Rey was getting antsy, and she crawled quietly through the space to see exactly what Han and Chewie were up against.

Through the grated floor of the ship, Finn

and Rey could see six gang members, all wearing red-and-black armored suits and carrying blasters.

As Han was trying to placate them, a second band docked with the ship and trapped Han, Chewbacca, and BB-8 in the middle of the corridor.

Rey wanted to see the new arrivals as well, so they crawled under the floor until they were near what Han was calling the Kanjiklub Gang. To her dismay, they were also heavily armed. The gang's leader, Tasu Leech, spoke in a language Finn couldn't understand.

"Your game is old," Bala-Tik said. "There's no one in the galaxy left for you to swindle." He glanced at BB-8, who was hiding behind Han's legs.

"That BB unit," said Bala-Tik. "The First Order is looking for one just like it . . . and two fugitives."

Finn and Rey froze, neither one daring to breathe.

They heard Han lie: "First I've heard of it."

Finn and Rey could hear the gang members starting to search the ship. They needed to move. But as they crawled under the floor, Rey stopped near a set of fuses.

"If we close the blast doors in that corridor, we can trap both groups!" Rey whispered.

"Close the blast doors?" Finn asked. "From here?"

"Resetting the fuses should do it," Rey said as she pushed various controls.

All of a sudden, the lights went out, a series of doors opened, and ghastly roars echoed through the ship.

"I've got a bad feeling about this," Han said above Rey and Finn.

"Oh, no," said Rey.

"What?" Finn didn't understand.

"Wrong fuses," Rey answered.

Above them, utter chaos erupted as three angry rathtars broke loose onto the already tense scene.

"Kill them!" they heard Bala-Tik shout. "And take the droid."

Rey and Finn began a headlong crawl back to the landing bay. Above them, Finn could hear telltale sounds of a firefight. He hoped Han, Chewie, and BB-8 could make it back to the *Falcon*, but at that moment, Finn and Rey were the only ones without weapons on board a ship filled with rathtars and gang members.

"This was a mistake!" Finn yelled.

"Huge!" Rey agreed.

The two scrambled up through an unlocked hatch and began running down corridors, looking for a way back to the landing bay while keeping an eye out for rathtars.

"What do they look like?" Rey panted as they turned another corner and skidded to a stop.

A screaming gang member was in full retreat from a hissing rathtar, which was using its tentacles to fling itself down the hall.

Rey's hand flew to her mouth in horror.

"They look like that!" Finn said as he took Rey's arm and began to run. The pustule-covered body of the rathtar followed close behind, reaching its twelve long tentacles toward them.

"This way," Finn shouted, hoping against hope that the landing bay would be right around the corner.

"Are you sure?" Rey asked.

Finn only answered her with a scream.

One of the rathtar's tentacles had wrapped around him, and it was now pulling him away from her down corridor after corridor.

Finn heard Rey screaming his name, but there was nothing he could do except scream her name back. The rathtar had him, and any moment it was going to swallow him in one gulp.

But as quickly as the nightmare had started, it was over. A set of heavy doors clamped together, severing several of the rathtar's tentacles. Finn was free!

He stood up in a panic, shaking the severed limbs to the floor, amazed that he was still alive and not missing any limbs of his own.

Around the corner dashed Rey.

He looked wild-eyed at her. "It had me! But the door—"

She interrupted him. "That was lucky!"

Rey and Finn managed to find the landing bay. Han, BB-8, and an injured Chewie were waiting for them by the *Falcon*, and they all dashed up the entry ramp. Han took command and began issuing orders.

"You"—he pointed at Rey—"close the door behind us."

"You," he said to Finn, shoving Chewie toward him and running toward the cockpit, "take care of Chewie."

Finn dragged the pained Wookiee inside the ship and got him to lie down. His fur was singed from a blast on the shoulder. Finn needed to find some gauze.

"Hang on back there!" Han called.

"No problem!" Finn yelled back, tossing aside odd objects until he found the materials he needed.

But there *was* a problem. He had to bandage up a rather angry Wookiee.

"Chewie, come on!" Finn urged him. But Chewie made it clear that he didn't want to be bandaged.

"I need help with this giant hairy thing!" Finn yelled toward the cockpit.

"You hurt Chewie, you're going to deal with me," Han shouted back.

"Hurt him?" Finn exclaimed. "He almost killed me six times!"

Chewie grabbed hold of Finn's neck and pulled him close so Finn could get a good look at the Wookiee's fangs. "Which is fine," Finn added.

Lesson learned.

CHAPTER
11

ONCE HAN WAS SURE they were on the right trajectory at lightspeed, he left the cockpit.

"Move, ball," he said to BB-8 as he made his way through the ship to check on Chewie.

The Wookiee was clearly disappointed with himself over the gang fight.

Han reassured his friend. "No, don't say that. You did great. Just rest."

Then the pilot turned to Finn. "Good job, kid," he said sincerely. "Thanks."

"You're welcome," Finn replied as he leaned forward on a strange table. The table lit up when Finn touched it, and odd holographic figures appeared and started fighting one another. Chewie perked up from the corner of the room.

"So . . . fugitives, huh?" Han asked.

Finn decided it might be best to turn off the game for then.

Rey had joined them. "The First Order wants the map," she explained. "Finn is in the Resistance. I'm just a scavenger."

The lie haunted Finn. He was thankful that Han changed the subject by asking to see BB-8's map.

The little droid rolled to the center of the ship and projected the map for them to see.

"This map is not complete. It's just a piece," Han explained, bathed in the blue light of the hologram. "Ever since Luke disappeared, people have been looking for him."

"Why did he leave?" asked Rey.

"He was training a new generation of Jedi," Han replied. "One boy, an apprentice, turned against him and destroyed it all. Luke felt responsible. He just walked away from everything."

"Do you know what happened to him?" Finn asked.

"A lot of rumors. Stories. People that knew him best think he went looking for the first Jedi Temple."

"The Jedi *were* real," Rey said, her eyes widening.

"I used to wonder about that myself," Han admitted. "Thought it was a bunch of mumbo jumbo. A magical power holding together good and evil, the dark side and the light? Crazy thing is, it's true. The Force. The Jedi. All of it. It's all true."

Finn and Rey were spellbound by Han's words.

"You want my help? You're getting it," said the smuggler. "Gonna see an old friend, she'll get your droid home. This is our stop."

The *Millennium Falcon* came out of

lightspeed over a beautiful blue-and-green planet dotted with white clouds.

As they soared over the lush world, Rey gaped out the window. "I didn't know there was this much green in the whole galaxy."

Finn was too worried about his own predicament to appreciate the scenic view. What would the *real* Resistance fighters say when they figured out he was a fraud? What if the First Order was waiting for them wherever Han was landing the ship?

The *Falcon* touched down near an ancient castle overlooking a lake. Rey left the ship immediately to take in the beauty, but Finn hung back when he noticed that Han was arming himself.

"Hey, Solo," Finn started, putting on his most Resistance-y voice, "I'm not sure what we're getting into here. . . ."

Han stopped and turned around to glare at Finn. "Did you just call me 'Solo'?"

"Sorry, Han . . . Mr. Solo," Finn continued.

"You should know, I'm a big deal in the Resistance, which puts a real target on my back. Are there any conspirators here? Like First Order sympathizers?"

"Listen, 'Big Deal,' you've got another problem," Han replied. "Women always figure out the truth. Always."

He shoved a blaster into Finn's hands and headed down the ramp to talk to Rey.

How did Han know he was lying?

Finn hated lying to Rey.

He wouldn't be able to face her when she found out the truth about him. Maybe it would be better if they just went their separate ways. . . .

A short hike later, Han, Finn, Rey, and BB-8 were approaching the gigantic stone castle.

"Solo, why are we here, again?" Finn asked.

"To get your droid on a clean ship," Han replied.

"Clean?" Rey didn't understand what he meant.

"You think it was luck that Chewie and I found the *Falcon*?" Han retorted. "If we can find it on our scanners, the First Order is not far behind."

A gigantic stone statue of a female alien loomed over the group as they made their way through the castle courtyard.

"Wanna get Beebee-Ate to the Resistance? Maz Kanata is our best bet," Han said.

"We can trust her, right?" Finn was still apprehensive about the pit stop.

"Relax, kid," said Han, brushing aside Finn's concern. "She's run this watering hole for a thousand years."

As they approached the door, Han turned around and gave Finn and Rey some advice. "Maz is a bit of an acquired taste, so let me do the talking, and whatever you do, don't stare."

"At what?" Finn and Rey asked in unison.

"Any of it . . ." Han warned.

Finn couldn't believe his eyes as they stepped into the dimly lit cantina. Aliens and humanoids of all shapes and sizes milled about the stone room. Music filled the hall, and the scent of food hung thick in the air. During all the excitement, Finn hadn't realized just how hungry he had become.

Across the room, a short alien wearing large goggles, bangles, and beads swiveled around on the spot. "Han Solo!" she bellowed above the crowd, as though she had sensed rather than seen his arrival.

The music stopped, a glass shattered, and all eyes turned toward the new party.

"Oh, boy," Han grumbled to himself. Then, much louder, he called out, "Hey, Maz."

Maz approached them with a serious look in her eyes. "Where's my boyfriend?"

Rey and Finn exchanged looks of confusion.

"Chewie's working on the *Falcon*," Han explained.

"I like that Wookiee," said Maz. "I assume you need something. Desperately," the alien continued. "Let's get to it."

CHAPTER
12

MAZ TREATED FINN, REY, AND HAN
to a great feast. In return, they informed her
about BB-8's precious cargo.

"A map!" Maz exclaimed. "To Skywalker
himself?" She laughed and then pointed at Han.
"You're right back in the mess!"

"Maz, I need you to get this droid to Leia."

The alien seemed to consider the idea for
only a second before firmly saying no. "You've
been running away from this fight for too long,"
Maz urged him.

Then Maz spoke Han's name and something
in a language Finn couldn't understand before

finally telling Han that he needed to go home.

"Leia doesn't want to see me," said Han.

"Please," Finn interjected, trying to get things back on track, "we came here for your help."

"What fight?" Rey asked Maz earnestly.

"The *only* fight, against the dark side." Maz explained, "Through the ages, I've seen evil take many forms. The Sith. The Empire. Today, it is the First Order. Their shadow spreading across the galaxy. We must face them. Fight them. All of us."

Finn had heard enough. He was the only person there who knew the terrible destructive power of the First Order.

"There is no fight against the First Order—not one we can win," Finn stated. "Look around! There's no chance we haven't been recognized already. I bet you the First Order is on their way right—"

Finn stopped midsentence, distracted by Maz, who was adjusting her goggles and staring intently into his eyes.

"What's this?" Finn asked. "What are you doing?"

Then Maz climbed up on the table and started crawling toward him. Brushing aside the plates of food, she kept her eyes locked on Finn. BB-8 was startled when a cup bounced off his head.

Finn was startled, too. "Solo, what is she doing?"

"I don't know," Han answered. "But it ain't good."

"If you live long enough, you see the same eyes in different people," Maz observed. "I'm looking at the eyes of a man who wants to run."

Finn couldn't believe it. Who was this lady to try to tell him who he was? "You don't know a thing about me. Where I'm from, what I've seen. You don't know the First Order like I do. They'll slaughter us. We all need to run."

Maz crawled back to her seat.

"You see those two?" Maz pointed to some pirates in a far corner. "They'll trade work for transportation to the Outer Rim. There, you can disappear."

"Finn!" Rey interjected.

Finn looked at Rey. He didn't want to leave her. But he *really* didn't want to face the First Order.

"Come with me," Finn pleaded.

"What about Beebee-Ate? We're not done yet," she said. "We have to get him back to your base."

The lie.

He couldn't avoid it.

Finn looked Rey in the eyes and said, "I can't."

He stood up, gingerly offering the blaster to Han, though he hoped the man wouldn't need it back.

"Keep it, kid," Han said, as if reading Finn's thoughts.

Finn looked at Rey one last time and walked away.

He managed to keep himself under control as he made his way across the cantina. He sat down at the table Maz had directed him to and a few moments later had negotiated passage to the Outer Rim. He would soon board a modified freighter called the *Meson Martinet* to work in the service of Captain Sidon Ithano and his peg-legged first mate, Quiggold. But Rey walked up, looking somehow even more upset than she had back on Jakku when she thought he was a thief. Finn was glad she didn't have her staff.

"What are you doing?" Rey spat.

"Don't leave without me," Finn urged the pirates before following Rey to a quieter part of the hall.

"You can't just go," said Rey. "I won't let you."

"I'm not who you think I am," Finn replied. He really didn't want to tell her his secret. She would never be able to look at him the same way.

"Finn, what are you talking about?" Rey clearly wouldn't let him off easy.

"I'm not Resistance," Finn confessed. "I'm not a hero. I'm a stormtrooper."

Her betrayed look cut him to his core, but she had wanted the truth, so he was going to tell her the whole truth.

"Like all of them, I was taken from a family I'll never know," he said, "and raised to do one thing."

The weight of the past few days rushed back on him, from the death of Slip to his escape with Poe. He took a deep breath and continued speaking.

"But my first battle? I made a choice. I wasn't going to kill for them. So I ran. Right into you. And you looked at me like no one ever had. I was ashamed of what I was. But I'm done with the First Order. I'm never going back."

Suddenly, he found it hard to swallow, much less to speak. "Rey, come with me."

She held his gaze. "Don't go."

And that was that. She wouldn't go. He

couldn't stay. There was only one thing left to say. "Take care of yourself. Please."

Finn turned and headed back to the two pirates. With quiet resignation, he followed Captain Sidon Ithano and First Mate Quiggold to the door and stepped outside.

CHAPTER
13

FINN WAS HAULING the last of his new ship's supplies on board when he heard screams coming from the castle. He looked up and saw a bright red vein cutting across the blue sky. He stopped dead in his tracks.

Finn knew exactly what that red streak was. It was a blast coming from the First Order's deadliest weapon: the Starkiller. The Starkiller had the power to incinerate planets, and the blast in the sky indicated that the First Order had decided to put it to use.

Finn ran to find his friends. They were all in danger. He needed to help them.

A crowd had gathered outside the castle, including Han and Chewie.

"The First Order. They've done it," said Finn.

He scanned the crowd, but he couldn't find the one person he wanted more than anything to be safe. "Where's Rey?"

Han didn't know where she was. Finn was about to run into the forest to find her, but Maz grabbed his hand before he could sprint off.

Maz dragged Finn, Han, and Chewie back to her castle. She led them down a long corridor to a room containing a small wooden box.

"I've had this for ages," Maz said. "Kept it locked away."

She lifted the lid of the box and pulled out a sleek silver object.

Han seemed shocked. "Where did you get that?"

"A good question," Maz replied, "for another time."

Then she held out the object to Finn. The alien urged him. "Take it! Find your friend!"

Finn accepted the gift just as blasts rocked the castle walls around them. He could hear the screams of First Order TIE fighters.

"Those beasts!" Maz cried. "They're here!"

Finn, Han, Chewie, and Maz ran through the crumbling castle, dodging falling debris as they made their way outside. Utter chaos awaited them.

TIE fighters leveled the castle with just a few blasts. Stormtroopers were flocking to the wreckage. Han and Chewie wasted little time before they began to trade shots with the troopers.

Maz looked at Finn. "Rey and Beebee-Ate, they need you. Now go," she yelled above the explosions.

But Finn no longer had the blaster Han had given him.

"I need a weapon," he shouted back.

Maz pulled his wrist up in the air and placed it in front of his face, his hand still gripping the strange gift she had given him. "You have one!"

She pointed to a stud on the object, and when Finn touched it, a bright blue electric blade flared to life.

Wading into the invading stormtroopers, Finn found that their armor was no match for his lightsaber. There was nothing out there that could stop him, Finn thought as he defeated trooper after trooper, but then he stopped short.

Standing in front of him was a stormtrooper carrying a riot control baton. Even though the stormtroopers' armor made them indistinguishable, Finn knew it was Nines the moment he saw him.

"Traitor!" Nines snarled as he swung his baton at Finn's unprotected head. Sparks flew as Finn blocked it with his lightsaber and took a step back. Nines slammed his baton into Finn's lightsaber again and again.

Finn didn't want to fight his old friend. But he had no choice. Nines stood for everything Finn hated about the First Order. The pair fought, dealing each other blow after blow. They were evenly matched until Nines was able to land a hit with his baton. Finn flew backward, knocked clean off his feet.

Nines walked toward Finn. He was panting heavily and there was zero trace of compassion in his swagger. Finn looked up at his former friend as FN-2199 raised his weapon for a death blow.

But it never came.

Instead, Nines had been blasted backward himself. Rolling over, Finn saw Han running toward him, Chewbacca's bowcaster in hand and the Wookiee trailing not far behind.

"You okay, Big Deal?" Han hauled him to his feet.

"Thanks," Finn managed to say.

"Don't move!" crackled a voice behind them.

With no way out, Finn, Han, and Chewbacca were forced to surrender their weapons.

As the stormtroopers marched them toward

a transport, a roar rose over the nearby lake. It was a fleet of X-wings!

"It's the Resistance!" Han shouted.

Led by a black-and-orange X-wing, the Resistance pilots quickly took care of the TIE fighters buzzing above where Maz's castle had once stood, and soon turned to picking off stormtroopers on the ground.

Han, Finn, and Chewie were free!

"Quick!" Han instructed as they gathered their weapons once more and fought their way through the battle.

Finn looked back at the sky, where the black-and-orange X-wing was taking out TIE after TIE. It was almost a one-man show up there. Finn had never seen that kind of flying before.

As he ran through the battle, he saw something that stopped his heart. It was Kylo Ren. And he was carrying Rey! He was taking her aboard his shuttle!

"No!" Finn yelled as he darted across the

battlefield. He *needed* to get to Rey before that shuttle took off!

But he was too late.

"Rey!" Finn shouted as the shuttle rose off the ground and headed into the sky.

Finn ran back to where Han and Chewie were standing.

"He took her!" Finn gasped. "Did you see that? He took her. She's gone."

But Han's mind seemed a million parsecs away. "Yeah, yeah, I know," he said, pushing his way past Finn to walk toward the door of a Resistance shuttle that had just landed.

Finn looked at Chewie for answers, but Chewie just gave him a roar as he followed Han. Both Han and Chewie were clearly eager to see whoever was inside that ship.

CHAPTER
14

THE PERSON IN THE SHIP turned out
to be another famous war hero, General Leia
Organa. Finn learned that she also happened
to be Han's wife—whom he hadn't seen in some
time—as well as Luke Skywalker's sister.

Once they reached the Resistance base, Finn
left the *Millennium Falcon* and walked about in
a haze.

He didn't belong there.

And where was Rey?

He needed to get to Rey!

BB-8 distracted Finn from his thoughts when
he eagerly rolled by, beeping and chirping wildly

as he charged down a row of X-wings.

The ace pilot of the black-and-orange X-wing was climbing out of his ship and seemed to be just as thrilled to see the little droid as BB-8 was to see him.

Finn couldn't believe his eyes. The pilot was Poe Dameron!

Finn and Poe charged at each other and hugged, each equally shocked to see the other standing in front of him.

"Poe Dameron!" Finn shouted. "You're alive?"

"Buddy! So are you!" Poe replied.

Finn was still confused. "What happened to you?"

Poe punched him in the arm. "What happened? I got thrown from the crash. I woke up at night, no you, no ship, no nothing!"

BB-8 rolled up alongside them.

"Beebee-Ate said you saved him," Poe continued.

"No no no, it wasn't just me." Finn tried to explain. But Poe wasn't listening.

"You completed my mission, Finn, I—" Poe was distracted. "That's my jacket."

Finn started to take it off, but Poe wouldn't let him. "Keep it, it suits you," said Poe. "You're a good man, Finn."

No, Finn thought. He was not a good man. He had let Kylo Ren take Rey.

Then Finn had another thought.

"Poe," Finn said, grabbing his friend's shoulder, "I need your help."

Finn followed Poe as they ran down stone steps to the heart of the Resistance base. Various machines and diagrams filled the space, and fighters and leaders buzzed this way and that.

Finn worried what all those fearless, noble people would do when they found out who he really was—or who he had been, Finn thought, correcting himself.

Poe ran right up to General Leia Organa. "I'm sorry to interrupt," he said. "This is Finn. He needs to talk to you."

"And I need to talk to him," the general replied, turning to Finn. "That was incredibly brave what you did. Renouncing the First Order? Saving this man's life?"

Finn was undoubtedly surprised by her warm words, but it wasn't a time for compliments. "Thank you, ma'am, but a friend of mine was taken prisoner."

"Han told me about the girl," said General Organa with sadness in her eyes. "I'm sorry."

Poe interjected. "Finn's familiar with the weapon that destroyed the Hosnian system. He worked on the base."

"We're desperate for anything you can tell us," the general pleaded.

"That's where my friend was taken," said Finn. "I've got to get there fast."

"And I will do everything I can to help," General Organa promised. "But first you need to tell us all you know."

The Resistance's high command had gathered to discuss the plan. One of the X-wing pilots had finished a reconnaissance flight, and the data he had collected confirmed what Finn had told them.

As Poe displayed the acquired images, gasps could be heard from the veterans around the room. The weapon was massive, built into a planet, easily dwarfing the famed Death Star the Empire had created years before. While Finn had never seen it used, his time on the Starkiller base had helped him understand exactly how it worked.

"It uses the power of the sun," Finn explained. "As the weapon is charged, the sun is drained until it disappears."

"The First Order . . ." Leia interrupted, reading a report an anxious officer had just pressed into her hands. "They're charging the weapon again. Now." She hesitated, as if she didn't want to read further. "Our system is the next target," she added quietly.

That news froze almost everyone in the room—except for Han, of course.

"So," he drawled, "how do we blow it up?"

He smirked at the gaping looks he was getting from the Resistance admirals and generals. "There's always a way to do that," he reminded them.

"Han's right," General Organa agreed.

It took a second for them to process Han's challenge, and then one of the admirals spoke up. "In order for *that* amount of power to be contained, that base has to have some kind of thermal oscillator. . . ."

Finn knew exactly what the man was talking about and, more important, where it was. If the Resistance pilots could destroy the thermal oscillator using their X-wings, they could at least destabilize the weapon and maybe even destroy the planet!

But first, Admiral Ackbar reminded them, the base's shields had to be taken care of. Han turned to Finn. "Kid, you worked there. What do you got?"

Finn almost told the truth: that he had no idea how to disable the shields. But then he realized that might be his only chance to rescue Rey.

"I can disable the shields," Finn said confidently. "But I have to *be* there, on the planet."

Poe ran through the plan. "So we disable the shields. We take out the oscillator, and we blow up their big gun."

And rescue Rey, Finn thought.

CHAPTER
15

FINN, HAN, AND CHEWIE trudged across
a snowy plain on the Starkiller base. Han had
gotten them on the First Order base undetected,
but his high-speed approach had crash-landed
the *Falcon* in the snow.

Chewie carried a backpack full of explosives,
but they would only work from inside the walls.
Overhead, the sun was flickering as a giant
blinding beam of energy poured into a chasm in
the base. Finn knew they didn't have much time.
"The flooding tunnel is over that ridge. We'll get
in that way."

Han looked incredulously at Finn. "What was

your job when you were based here?" he asked suspiciously.

Finn looked back at him sheepishly. "Sanitation."

"*Sanitation?*" Han repeated. He shoved Finn against a cold metal wall. "Then how do you know how to disable the shields?"

Finn looked earnestly at Han. "I don't. I'm just here to get Rey."

"People are counting on us," Han scolded. "The galaxy is counting on us!"

"Solo, we'll figure it out!" Finn replied. "We'll use the Force!"

"That's not how the Force works!" Han groaned.

Chewie let out a groan of his own.

"Oh, really?" Han replied. "*You're* cold?"

Finn turned and walked toward the base. "Come on."

It turned out sanitation wasn't anything to scoff at. Finn quickly led them inside the base undetected. But Han knew their good fortune wasn't going to last.

"The shields?" He looked at Finn.

"I have an idea about that," Finn replied as he ran down the corridor.

A few minutes later, the three Resistance fighters had concealed themselves in the shadows and were waiting to ambush Captain Phasma. Chewie leaped out, grabbed Phasma, and pulled her into the narrow corridor.

Finn had dreamed about that moment.

"Do you remember me?" he asked.

"Eff-Enn-Two-One-Eight-Seven," she said. Finn could hear the hatred in her voice.

"Not anymore," he replied. "The name's Finn, and I'm in charge." Finn continued to taunt her. "I'm in charge now, Phasma. I'm in charge!"

"Bring it down," Han whispered in his ear. "Bring it down."

"Follow me," Finn ordered.

"You *want* me to blast that bucket off your head?" Finn sounded deadly serious.

They had found a workstation and now they just needed Phasma to do their work for them.

"Lower the shields," Finn ordered.

"You're making a big mistake," Phasma replied.

"Do it!" Finn commanded.

Chewie backed him up with a roar.

As Phasma pushed a few buttons, Finn looked at Han. "Solo, if this works, we're not going to have a lot of time to find Rey."

"Don't worry, kid." Han reassured him with a half smile. "We won't leave here without her."

A few moments later, Phasma stood up from the workstation. The deed was done. The shields were down. But she wasn't going to go without a fight.

"You can't be so stupid as to think this will be easy," she snarled. "My troops will storm this block and kill you all."

"I disagree," said Finn plainly, turning to Han. "What do we do with her?"

Han had been in that situation before. "Is there a garbage chute? A trash compactor?"

Finn smiled. "Yeah, there is."

Sanitation for the win.

After they dropped Phasma in the trash, Finn, Chewie, and Han continued their search through the base.

"We'll use the charges to blow that blast door," Finn instructed. "I'll go in and draw fire, but I'm gonna need cover."

"Sure you're up for this?" Han asked.

Finn made it clear that, *no*, in fact he was *not* up for it, but it was his only choice.

"I'll go in and try to find Rey," continued Finn. "The troopers will be on our tail. We have to be ready for that."

But it didn't seem like Han was listening to him anymore; he was just nodding along and looking over Finn's shoulder.

Finn was frustrated and asked what Han was doing. "I'm trying to come up with a plan," Finn reminded him.

Han used his blaster to motion behind Finn.

When Finn turned around, he understood why Han no longer cared about his plan.

Rey was climbing right outside the window!

"You all right?" Han asked Rey after they had reunited.

"Yeah," Rey replied, still shocked to see them there.

"Good," said Han.

"What happened to you, did he hurt you?" Finn was worried. He knew how evil Kylo Ren could be. He knew she had been in grave danger. Then again, he had also learned how tough Rey was. Maybe it had been an even match after all?

"Finn, what are you doing here?" Rey asked.

"We came back for you," Finn explained.

Chewie chimed in, but as usual, Finn couldn't understand him.

"What'd he say?" Finn asked Rey.

"That it was your idea," Rey answered, pulling Finn close for a hug. "Thank you."

Finn was happy to be with her again, but something still troubled him.

"How did you get away?" he asked her.

"I can't explain it," she whispered in his ear. "And you wouldn't believe it!"

Han rudely pushed in on them. "Escape now," he ordered. "Hug later."

Han, Chewie, Rey, and Finn ran across the snowy base, with X-wings and TIE fighters battling above them and the sun growing dimmer and dimmer by the moment. The Resistance was running out of time.

"They're in trouble," Han said. "We can't leave." He turned to Chewie. "My friend's got a bag full of explosives. Let's use 'em."

Finn's knowledge of the base and Rey's mechanical prowess got Han and Chewie inside the oscillator chamber with the explosives. But when Finn and Rey saw how close the sun was to extinction, they knew they needed to go into the chamber themselves to help.

Finn and Rey reached an upper door to the oscillator chamber, but something wasn't right.

Han was on a catwalk far below, walking toward Kylo Ren!

Why was he walking *toward* the dark warrior?

Finn and Rey watched as Kylo and Han spoke to each other. They couldn't hear what the men were saying, but the conversation seemed to last a lifetime. Kylo even took off his helmet.

And that was when Finn saw it: the resemblance between the two men.

It all became clear, though it made zero sense. Han was Kylo's father.

Han and Kylo were now just a few
centimeters from each other.

From high above the catwalk, Finn saw
Kylo drop his helmet, then offer his weapon
to his father just as the last ray of sunshine
disappeared from the sky outside.

But instead of letting Han take the weapon,
Kylo ignited the blade.

"No!" Finn and Rey shrieked. Chewie,
who'd been watching from another part of the
chamber, let out a moan of sadness.

The smuggler fell, lifeless, from the catwalk
into the darkness below.

CHAPTER
16

FINN AIMED HIS BLASTER AT KYLO,
intending to send him falling right behind Han.
But Chewie beat him to the punch. With an
anguished roar, Chewie used his bowcaster to
send a blast right to Kylo's side. The warrior was
hurt, but not fatally.

Chewie released shot after shot, taking out
Kylo's stormtroopers, before detonating the
explosives he had set with Han. The oscillator
chamber filled with flames!

Kylo looked up from where he was on the
catwalk, making eye contact with Finn.

Finn and Rey needed to run.

They scrambled out of the chamber and ran across the darkened planet's snowy surface, fleeing toward nearby woods. Finn's only thought was to get back to the *Falcon*. If the Resistance's plans went as designed, they had just a few minutes to make it off the planet and escape its destruction.

But the angry hiss of a lightsaber stopped Finn and Rey in their tracks. Kylo Ren limped out from behind some trees ahead of them. His red lightsaber threw evil shadows across his face. He glared darkly at the two of them, dragging his lightsaber blade on the ground next to him.

"We're not done yet," Kylo snarled.

Despite Kylo's obvious injuries, Finn knew they would never outrun the warrior and his dark powers. Looking at Rey, he saw her hand tighten around the handle of a stormtrooper blaster she had picked up along the way.

"You're a monster," she spat.

"It's just us now. Han Solo can't save you now,"

Kylo sneered, working himself into a fury by pounding on the wound Chewie had given him.

Without warning, Rey snapped up her blaster and aimed, but using only his mind, Kylo managed to rip the blaster from Rey's grasp and fling her into a nearby tree like a rag doll.

"*Rey!*" Finn yelled, tossing his own blaster to the ground as he ran to where she had fallen.

He cradled her head. She was still breathing, but he couldn't tell how badly she was hurt.

Finn's mind went dark with anger.

"Traitor!" Kylo screamed at Finn, swinging his red blade back and forth.

In reply, Finn reached down to his waist, unclipped his own lightsaber, and watched the blue blade ignite.

Kylo froze in shock at the sight of the weapon. "That lightsaber"—he pointed his red blade at Finn—"it belongs to me!"

"Come get it," said Finn before charging at Kylo with an angry guttural yell.

Kylo turned and slashed, but Finn was able

to deflect and then counterattack, pushing the injured man back. Kylo lunged at him again, pinning him up against a tree and slowly touching the blade to Finn's chest, burning through Poe's jacket.

Finn yelled out in pain.

From the corner of his eye, he thought he saw Rey stir. Was she all right?

Finn managed to push Kylo off and regain control of the duel. He cut and parried, some of his First Order training allowing him to gain a slight advantage, and he was even able to tag Kylo on the shoulder with a minor strike.

Then Kylo charged, began slashing with animal ferocity, and managed to knock Finn's lightsaber out of his hands. The precious weapon flew across the snow. Finn tried to run for the weapon, but Kylo punched him, and when Finn stumbled on his feet, Kylo dragged his lightsaber across Finn's back, sending him to the ground in agony.

The pain was like a fire in Finn's mind as he felt his muscles grow weak and limp. The heat from his body melted the snow that was collecting around him. He thought he could hear the sound of lightsabers igniting once more.

But the pain was all consuming, and more and more of his body was getting numb. A darkness was falling over him; he couldn't fight it anymore.

Rey, he thought before his mind went blank.

Rey was his only hope.